Circus Play

Circus Play

written *by* Anne Laurel Carter
illustrated by Joanne Fitzgerald

ORCA BOOK PUBLISHERS

Everyone calls my house The Big Top.
Kids knock at the window, wanting to play.
Today it's Dan and Nisha, little Stuie holding his bear.

"Come in," I call.

Their wide eyes stare. "Is that really your mom?"
"Don't mind her," I say. "Let's watch TV."
They take ringside seats.

Mom wears her sparkle suit. Her trapeze hangs from the ceiling.
She jumps up and . . .

spins a windmill circle through the air.

"Ooh, she's floating . . ."
   ". . . like a mermaid . . ."
      ". . . like my goldfish, Arabella."

"Shhh," I say. "You'll miss the TV show."
Why can't I have an ordinary mom?
Mom curls up and . . .

rolls like a monkey.

Stuie sees my Circus Costume Box. "Can I look?"
Dan and Nisha squeeze behind him.
I hope they don't find the clown suits.

Yesterday, the kids left a terrible mess,
juggling pins and mile-long scarves everywhere.

Mom flips headfirst to the floor and . . .
hangs by her toes.

The curtain parts . . . a little lion prances out,

a big elephant behind him.
Mom's back on the bar.
Below her I see
a lion tamer in snappy black boots.
The lion paws the ground . . . charges.

"Look out!" roars the elephant.
The lion tamer whips off her red sash. "Toro! Toro!" she cries.
"Wait!" I hold up my hand. "A circus doesn't have bullfights."

But my mom sparkles at them, waves . . .

a flag in the breeze.

I grab the red sash and whip it. *Flick, flack.*
"You're supposed to be a lion tamer and a lion!" *Flack, flick.*

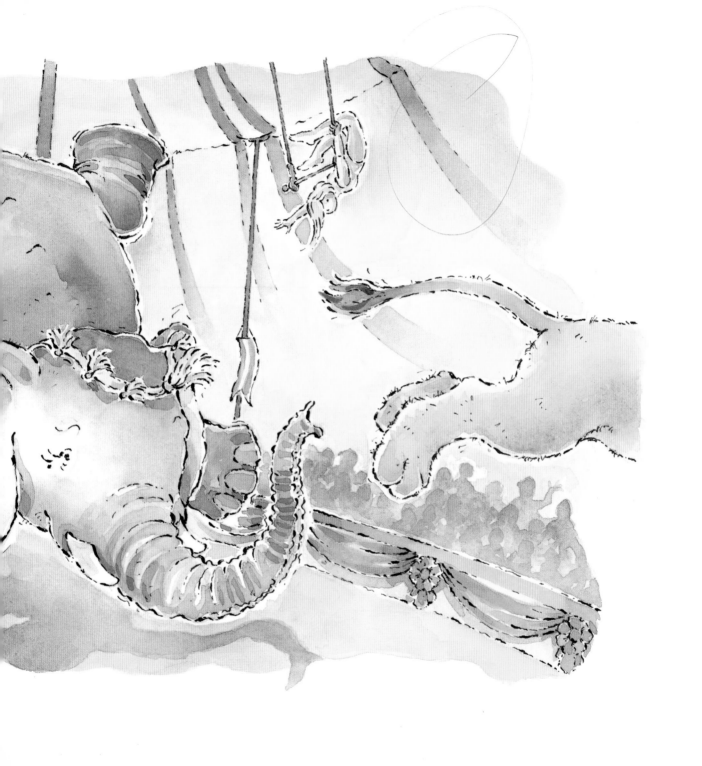

Oh-oh. The elephant has scared the lion.

The lion tamer climbs on the elephant's back.
"He's in the jungle. Let's hunt him down."

The hunter kicks . . .

"Ow!" roars the elephant, collapsing to the floor.
"A circus doesn't have safaris." I'm trying not to watch them.
A jungle spills everywhere as the lion escapes.

Overhead, Mom spins around the world.
The lion runs up the stairs,
the elephant and hunter close on his tail.
"Help!" he yells. "I'm stuck!"
"Push!" grunts the elephant. "Point your arms, Stuie.
Head for outer space!"

I turn off the TV. "A circus has cannons, not rocket ships."

"Three, two, one, blast-off!"

From one rope to another, my mom . . .

shoots the moon
while a little lion flies past.

I catch him. We land on the sofa.
Stuie and his bear grin up at me. "Want to play?"

Above us
my mom's a banana split.

I wonder if they can come back tomorrow.
"I know a circus way to set the table. Want to see?"
They stop at the doorway. Their wide eyes stare.

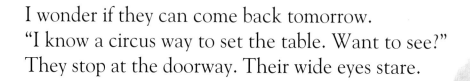

I flick the red tablecloth, *whip, snap,*
     throw out the plates, *zip, zap,*
         and light the candles, *puff.*

My extra-ordinary mom reaches out her hands and I
shoot like a bright star across the Big Top.

National Library of Canada Cataloguing in Publication Data
Carter, Anne, 1953-

Circus play .

ISBN: 1-55143-225-0

I. Fitzgerald, Joanne, 1956- II. Title.

PS8555.A7727C57 2002   jC813'.54   C2002-910504-8

PZ7.C2427Ci 2002

First published in the United States, 2002

Library of Congress Control Number: 2002105067

Summary: When Mom's trapeze act steals the show, the least her upstaged son can do is make sure that the child performers stay true to the grand traditions of the Big Top.

Teacher's guide available from Orca Book Publishers.

Orca Book Publishers gratefully acknowledges the support of its publishing programs provided by the following agencies: the Department of Canadian Heritage, the Canada Council for the Arts, and the British Columbia Arts Council.

Design by Christine Toller
Printed and bound in Hong Kong

IN CANADA:
Orca Book Publishers
PO Box 5626, Station B
Victoria, BC Canada
V8R 6S4

IN THE UNITED STATES:
Orca Book Publishers
PO Box 468
Custer, WA   USA
98240-0468

04 03 02 • 5 4 3 2 1

the end